W9-BXW-461

HISTORY SPEAKS
PICTURE BOOKS PLUS READER'S THEATER

John Greenwood's
JOURNEY TO
BUNKER HILL

BY **MARTY RHODES FIGLEY**

ILLUSTRATED BY **CRAIG ORBACK**

M MILLBROOK PRESS / MINNEAPOLIS

For Glenn Stelzer, another patriot who ran away from home when he was fifteen to fight for his country —MRF

To Lisa, for showing me the historical New England sites —CO

Text copyright © 2011 by Marty Rhodes Figley
Illustrations © 2011 by Craig Orback

Millbrook Press
A division of Lerner Publishing Group, Inc.
241 First Avenue North
Minneapolis, MN 55401 U.S.A.

Website address: www.lernerbooks.com

The illustrator gives special thanks to those who modeled for the various characters—most especially Evan Pengra Sult as John Greenwood and Jessica Silks as Mrs. Greenwood.

The images in this book are used with the permission of: © Cpenler/Dreamstime.com, p. 32; Library of Congress (LC-USZ62-56114), p. 33.

Library of Congress Cataloging-in-Publication Data

Figley, Marty Rhodes, 1948–
    John Greenwood's journey to Bunker Hill / by Marty Rhodes Figley ; illustrated by Craig Orback.
        p. cm. — (History speaks: picture books plus reader's theater)
    Includes bibliographical references.
    ISBN 978–1–58013–673–0 (lib. bdg. : alk. paper)
    1. Acting—Juvenile literature. 2. Greenwood, John, 1760–1819—Juvenile drama. 3. United States—History—Revolution, 1775–1783—Juvenile drama. 4. Readers' theater. I. Orback, Craig, ill. II. Title.
    PN2080.F53 2011
812'.6—dc22   2009050063

Manufactured in the United States of America
1 – BP – 7/15/10

CONTENTS

FALMOUTH (NOW PORTLAND, MAINE)

Mid-May 1775

On a quiet Sunday morning, John Greenwood decided to run away. He knew his uncle would not miss him for a while.

John tucked his fife, a small but loud flute, in his pocket. He counted seven coins. It was all the money he owned in the world. John had earned it playing his fife when the local militia marched. The militiamen were the town's volunteer soldiers.

He bundled three shirts and an extra pair of socks inside a big handkerchief. And he added his sword for protection. John was off to Boston, Massachusetts, to see his parents, brothers, and sister. He had not seen them for two long years.

John had been living with his uncle Thales Greenwood in Falmouth. His parents sent him there when he was thirteen years old to learn how to make furniture.

A week earlier, as John worked quietly alongside his uncle, he had almost asked for permission to leave. But he was sure Uncle Thales would not allow him to go. And then Uncle Thales might guess that John would try to leave anyway.

There was serious trouble in Boston. John worried that British soldiers might harm his family. He wanted to be near them. But first, he had a few days of walking to do. Boston was 150 miles away.

In April, hundreds of British soldiers had left Boston, heading toward the towns of Lexington and Concord. They planned to destroy the colonists' supply of ammunition and guns. American militiamen at Lexington and Concord tried to stop them. The first shots of war were fired.

Town bells rang across New England. Militiamen came from near and far. They chased the British solders all the way back to Boston. The British government was furious. Soon thousands of British soldiers poured into Boston to keep the colonists under control.

John was not surprised war had finally arrived. Many American colonists were tired of the British government telling them what to do. They wanted their own representatives to vote on the laws they lived by and the taxes they paid.

Now John was finally going home! He slipped out
of Uncle Thales's house before breakfast. With a light
heart, he jumped over the backyard fence. Sometimes
John ran. And sometimes, he trotted like a horse.

Men carrying muskets crowded the road. They, too,
were heading toward Boston. The colonists came from
farms and villages all over New England. They were
off to join the fight for their rights.

By evening, John had traveled almost forty
miles. The setting sun turned the sky gray
and gold. John's stomach rumbled with hunger.
    He stumbled across a fallen branch. Then he
heard a sound that made him jump.
    "Whoo, whoo!"
    "Just a noisy old owl," he told himself.

A welcome light shone through the trees. It came
from a tavern. John's mouth watered at the thought of
hot food. Inside, men were drinking rum and cider and
talking of war.

The tavern keeper looked John up and down. John had
just turned fifteen. But he was small for his age. He knew

"What brings you here, lad?" the tavern keeper asked.
John said, "I'm on my way to Boston to fight for my country."
The men cheered and patted John on the back.

13

The tavern keeper spotted the fife in John's pocket.
"Can you play us a tune?" he asked.
John said, "I've been playing since I was nine."

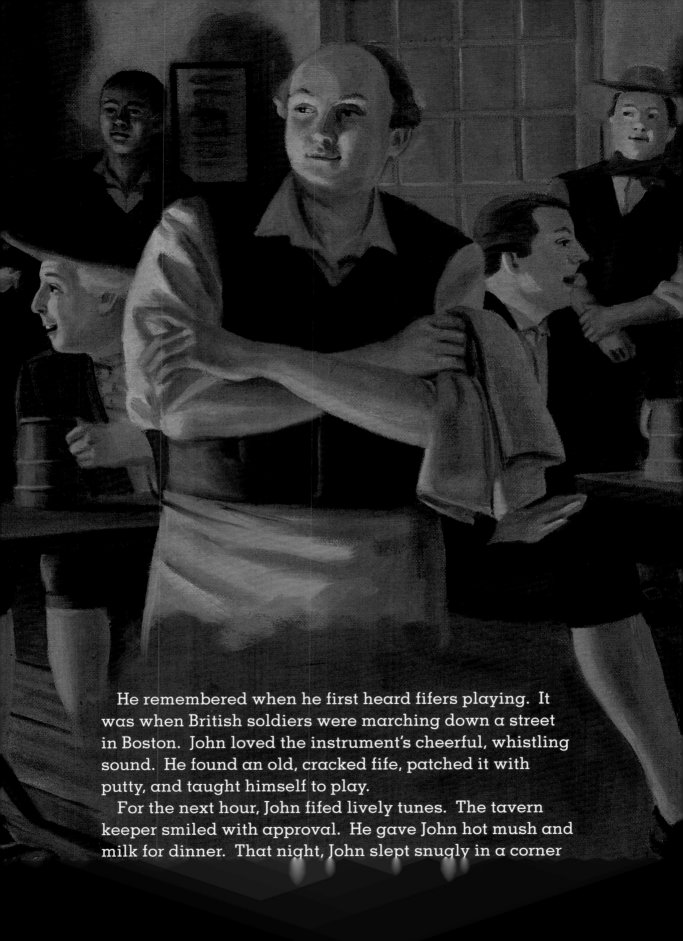

He remembered when he first heard fifers playing. It was when British soldiers were marching down a street in Boston. John loved the instrument's cheerful, whistling sound. He found an old, cracked fife, patched it with putty, and taught himself to play.

For the next hour, John fifed lively tunes. The tavern keeper smiled with approval. He gave John hot mush and milk for dinner. That night, John slept snugly in a corner

For the rest of his journey, John earned his keep at taverns along the way. Each night, he played for his supper and a place to sleep.

After walking four and a half days, John reached a narrow piece of land called the Charlestown Neck. It led to Charlestown, a small village that lay just across the river from Boston.

A colonist stood guard there.

"Do you have a pass?" the man asked.

John looked down at his dusty shoes. His feet ached badly.

"No," he muttered.

The guard said, "Lad, the war has begun. Our troops have surrounded the city. And the British Army is trapped inside." He winked. "We want to keep them in there."

"But I've traveled so far to see my family!" John said.

"You'll have to get a pass," said the guard. "Then you can take the Charlestown ferry across the river to Boston."

John tried to run past the man. Another guard caught him. John had to spend the night in the guardhouse.

The next day, John walked a few miles to Cambridge.
The town was the headquarters for American troops.
There, John found a general who gave him a pass.
He returned to Charlestown to catch the ferry to Boston.
   Hundreds of people crowded around the dock. They had
ridden the ferryboat from Boston to Charlestown. They
wanted to escape from Boston before the fighting began.

John showed the ferry keeper his pass.

"Sorry, lad," the ferry keeper said. "We aren't letting the British soldiers out of Boston. And they have decided they aren't letting anyone in."

John felt hot tears fill his eyes. After two years, he was so close to his parents. But he could not see them!

Within a few days, most citizens had also left Charlestown. The village was empty. John's pockets were empty too.

John went into a large tavern. He played a few tunes on his fife.

A militiaman invited John to sit across from him. He bought John a mug of cider.

"We need fifers," the man said. "Why don't you go to Cambridge and enlist in the army? You'll be paid eight dollars a month. You'll fife when the soldiers march. In camp, you'll play to cheer up the men and," he said with a smile, "to let them know it's time to wake up."

The man had John's full attention. He added, "Sometimes you'll even help the commanders during a battle by giving the men signals with your fife. Does that sound like something you can do, lad?"

John nodded. Yes, he would fife with all his might for his countrymen. They would drive the British Army out of Boston. Then John could see his family.

Early in the morning on June 17, John was
walking near Cambridge. He was now a fifer with
Captain Bliss's company and was on leave for the day.

John heard the great guns begin to boom in the
distance. The fighting had started! He ran back to
Cambridge to join his company. When John reached the
center of town, a man he knew stopped him.

"John, your mother is at my house," he said. "She
heard you enlisted. And she managed to get a pass to
come from Boston and visit you."

John found his mother in a house filled with crying children and frightened women. Mrs. Greenwood hugged John.

"I've missed you so, Johnny," she said.

They had only a moment to talk. John had to find his company. His mother would have to find a place to stay in Cambridge until she could safely return to Boston. John left the house and ran toward the sounds of battle. They seemed to be coming from Bunker Hill.

John saw signs of terror and confusion everywhere.
Soldiers carried men who had been hurt during the battle.
More wounded men rolled by on wagons. Their groans and
cries made John's hair stand on end.

"Oh, why did I enlist?" John thought to himself. "Why did
I think I could fight the British soldiers? They are the most
powerful army in the world!"

A tall black American soldier walked toward John. He had
a wound on his neck. Blood ran down his back.

As the soldier drew near, John asked, "Does it hurt?"

The soldier shrugged. "Not too much," he said. "I'm going to get a bandage put on it. Then I will return to battle."

His words cheered John. From that moment on, John decided he would try to act brave like that soldier.

John touched the fife in his pocket. He took a deep breath. Then he continued down the road to join the fight.

The battle was in Charlestown. John arrived in time to help the American militiamen, who had mostly gathered on Breed's Hill. Thousands of British soldiers began charging up the hill. The British fifers played as they charged. John and the other American fifers answered with their own battle tunes.

There were more British soldiers than Americans. The British also had better muskets and more of them.

But the American soldiers stayed calm. Their bravery amazed John. The men obeyed the commander who said, "Don't fire until you can see the whites of their eyes."

The Americans forced the charging British soldiers to turn back twice. The muskets sounded to John like the roll of one hundred drums. Smoke filled the air. And then the Americans ran out of gunpowder. They had to retreat. The British had won. John's company went back to Cambridge.

One month after the battle, John stood by his tent and stared. He saw his mother rushing toward him. One of the soldiers, Sergeant Mills, was with her.

"Oh, Johnny!" Mrs. Greenwood said, hugging him tightly.
"I thought you were killed during the Battle of Bunker Hill."
This time, John and his mother had a real visit. They talked
and talked, trying to make up for the two years they were apart.

Mrs. Greenwood kissed John good-bye. "I'll be going back to Boston now. I spoke to General Washington, and he gave me a pass." She hugged John again and said, "My brave boy, I'm so proud of you."

She turned to Sergeant Mills. "What shall I tell the British in Boston when I get back home? They will probably ask me questions about you."

Sergeant Mills grinned at John. "Tell them we are ready for them at any time they choose to come and attack us," he said.

John nodded in agreement. After Bunker Hill, he knew he could do anything.

Afterword

After the Battle of Lexington and Concord on April 19, 1775, the British soldiers returned to Boston. American troops surrounded them there.

On June 15, word came that the British Army was going to try to take the high ground around the city. On the night of June 16, Americans built defenses on Breed's Hill. It was close enough to Boston so that cannon balls could reach their targets in the city. Nearby Bunker Hill was higher than Breed's Hill, but it was too far from Boston. The next day, British troops attacked. The battle is called the Battle of Bunker Hill. But most of the fighting took place on Breed's Hill. A monument to remember the battle was later built on Breed's Hill.

More than one thousand British soldiers who fought were wounded or killed. Americans suffered around four hundred wounded or

BUNKER HILL MONUMENT

killed. The battle showed the British that the Americans were fierce fighters. The British realized they would not win the war quickly.

John Greenwood was a real person. He was born in Boston on May 17, 1760. He fifed for American soldiers at Bunker Hill. Later, he fifed for American troops in Montreal, Canada, and in New Jersey. John fought with George Washington in the Battle of Trenton on December 26, 1776.

JOHN GREENWOOD

In 1779, John joined the war at sea. The British captured his ship. He spent several months in a prison with a dungeon in Barbados, West Indies. After his release, John rejoined the fighting. Before the war ended, he was captured three more times. He always managed to escape.

John received only six months pay for his twenty months in the army. He never asked for more money. John was proud of the part he played in the fight for America's independence.

John's father was a dentist. John learned that profession from him. In 1784, John set up his own dental practice in New York City. He went on to become George Washington's favorite dentist. He made many of President Washington's false teeth, including ones made from hippopotamus ivory. Washington wrote to him, "I shall always prefer your services to that of any other in the line of your present profession."

In 1809, John Greenwood wrote about his war memories in "A Young Patriot in the American Revolution." He died on November 16, 1819, at the age of fifty-nine. John's memories were first published by his grandson Isaac 113 years later.

Performing Reader's Theater

Dear Student,

Reader's Theater is a dramatic reading. It is a little like a play, but you don't need to memorize your lines. Here are some tips that will help you do your best in a Reader's Theater performance.

BEFORE THE PERFORMANCE

- **Choose your part:** Your teacher may assign parts, or you may be allowed to choose your own part. The character you play does not need to be the same age as you. A boy can play the part of a girl, and a girl can play the part of a boy. That's why it's called acting!

- **Find your lines:** Your character's name is always the same color. The name at the bottom of each page tells you which character has the first line on the next page. If you are allowed to write on your script, highlight your lines. If you cannot write on the script, you may want to use sticky flags to mark your lines.

- **Check pronunciations of words:** If your character's lines include any words you aren't sure how to pronounce, check the pronunciation guide on page 45. If a word isn't there or you still aren't sure how to say it, check a dictionary or ask a teacher, librarian, or other adult.

- **Use your emotions:** Think about how your character feels in the story. If you imagine how your character feels, the audience will hear the emotion in your voice.

- **Use your imagination:** Think about how your character's voice might sound. For example, an old man's voice will sound different from a baby's voice. If you do change your voice, make sure the audience can still understand the words you are saying.

- **Practice your lines:** Even though you do not need to memorize your lines, you should still be comfortable reading them. Read your lines aloud often so they flow smoothly.

DURING THE PERFORMANCE

- **Keep your script away from your face but high enough to read:** If you cover your face with your script, you block your voice from the audience. If you have your script too low, you need to tip your head down farther to read it and the audience won't be able to hear you.

- **Use eye contact:** Good Reader's Theater performers look at the audience as much as they look at their scripts. If you look down, the sound of your voice goes down to the script and not out to the audience.

- **Speak clearly:** Make sure you are loud enough. Say all your words carefully. Be sure not to read too quickly. Remember, if you feel nervous, you may start to speak faster than usual.

- **Use facial expressions and gestures:** Your facial expressions and gestures (hand movements) help the audience know how your character is feeling. If your character is happy, smile. If your character is angry, cross your arms and be sure not to smile.

- **Have fun:** It's okay if you feel nervous. If you make a mistake, just try to relax and keep going. Reader's Theater is meant to be fun for the actors and the audience!

Cast of Characters

NARRATOR 1

NARRATOR 2

JOHN:
a fifteen-year-old boy

COLONIST GUARD:
a guard who checks people going into Boston

MILITIAMAN:
a citizen fighting with the American army

MRS. GREENWOOD:
John's mother

READER 1:
tavern keeper, man

READER 2:
ferry keeper, soldier, sergeant Mills

ALL BUT JOHN:
everyone except John and sound

SOUND:
This part has no lines.
The person in this role
is in charge of the sound effects.

The Script

NARRATOR 1: On a quiet Sunday morning in May 1775, John Greenwood decided to run away to Boston, Massachusetts, to see his parents, brothers, and sister. He had not seen them for two long years because he had been living with his uncle. He packed his fife, a small but loud flute, and seven coins. It was all the money he owned in the world.

NARRATOR 2: There was serious trouble in Boston. In April, hundreds of British soldiers had left Boston, heading toward the towns of Lexington and Concord. They planned to destroy the colonists' supply of ammunition and guns. American militiamen, or volunteer soldiers, at Lexington and Concord tried to stop them. The first shots of war were fired.

SOUND: [shot being fired]

NARRATOR 1: Militiamen chased the British solders all the way back to Boston. The British government was furious. Soon thousands of British soldiers poured into Boston to keep the colonists under control. Many American colonists were tired of the British government telling them what to do. They wanted their own representatives to vote on the laws they lived by and the taxes they paid.

JOHN: I'm finally going home! I'm very worried that British soldiers might harm my family. I want to be near them. But first, I have a few days of walking to do. Boston is 150 miles away.

Next Page — **NARRATOR 2**

NARRATOR 2: Men carrying muskets crowded the road. They, too, were heading toward Boston. The colonists came from farms and villages all over New England. They were off to join the fight for their rights.

NARRATOR 1: By evening, John had traveled almost forty miles. The setting sun turned the sky gray and gold. John's stomach rumbled with hunger. He stumbled across a fallen branch. Then he heard a sound that made him jump.

SOUND: [owl hooting]

JOHN: What was that? Oh, just a noisy old owl.

NARRATOR 2: A welcome light shone through the trees. It came from a tavern. John's mouth watered at the thought of hot food. Inside, men were drinking rum and cider and talking of war. The tavern keeper looked John up and down.

READER 1 (AS TAVERN KEEPER): What brings you here, lad?

JOHN: I'm on my way to Boston to fight for my country.

SOUND: [men cheering]

READER 1 (AS TAVERN KEEPER): Can you play us a tune on your fife?

JOHN: I've been playing since I was nine. I love the instrument's cheerful, whistling sound. I first heard fifers playing when British soldiers were marching down a street in Boston. I found an old, cracked fife, patched it with putty, and taught myself to play.

Next Page — **NARRATOR 1**

NARRATOR 1: For the next hour, John fifed lively tunes.

SOUND: [fife playing]

READER 1 (AS TAVERN KEEPER): You are a good fife player. How would you like some supper and a place to sleep for your playing?

NARRATOR 2: For the rest of his journey, John earned his keep at taverns along the way. Each night, he played for his supper and a place to sleep.

NARRATOR 1: After walking four and a half days, John reached a narrow piece of land called the Charlestown Neck. It led to Charlestown, a small village that lay just across the river from Boston. A colonist stood guard there.

COLONIST GUARD: Do you have a pass?

JOHN: No.

COLONIST GUARD: Lad, the war has begun. Our troops have surrounded the city. And the British Army is trapped inside. We want to keep them in there.

JOHN: But I've traveled so far to see my family!

COLONIST GUARD: You'll have to get a pass. Then you can take the Charlestown ferry across the river to Boston.

NARRATOR 2: John tried to run past the man. Another guard caught him. John had to spend the night in the guardhouse.

Next Page — **NARRATOR 1**

NARRATOR 1: The next day, John walked a few miles to Cambridge. The town was the headquarters for American troops. There, John found a general who gave him a pass. He returned to Charlestown to catch the ferry to Boston. Hundreds of people crowded around the dock. They had ridden the ferryboat from Boston to Charlestown. They wanted to escape from Boston before the fighting began.

JOHN: I have a pass to go to Boston.

READER 2 (AS FERRY KEEPER): Sorry, lad. We aren't letting the British soldiers out of Boston. And they have decided they aren't letting anyone in.

JOHN: After two years, I am so close to my parents. But I cannot see them!

NARRATOR 2: Within a few days, most citizens had also left Charlestown. The village was empty. John's pockets were empty too. John went into a large tavern. He played a few tunes on his fife.

SOUND: [fife playing]

MILITIAMAN: Come sit with me. Can I buy you a mug of cider?

JOHN: Yes, thank you.

Next Page — **MILITIAMAN**

MILITIAMAN: I am an American militiaman. We need fifers. Why don't you go to Cambridge and enlist in the army? You'll be paid eight dollars a month. You'll fife when the soldiers march. In camp, you'll play to cheer up the men and to let them know it's time to wake up. Sometimes you'll even help the commanders during a battle by giving the men signals with your fife. Does that sound like something you can do, lad?

JOHN: Yes, I will fife with all my might for my countrymen. We will drive the British Army out of Boston. Then I can see my family.

NARRATOR 1: Early in the morning on June 17, John was walking near Cambridge. He was now a fifer with Captain Bliss's company and was on leave for the day. John heard the great guns begin to boom in the distance.

SOUND: [guns booming]

JOHN: The fighting has started! I need to run back to Cambridge to join my company.

NARRATOR 2: When John reached the center of town, a man he knew stopped him.

READER 1 (AS MAN): John, your mother is at my house. She heard you enlisted. And she managed to get a pass to come from Boston and visit you.

NARRATOR 1: John found his mother in a house filled with crying children and frightened women. Mrs. Greenwood hugged John.

MRS. GREENWOOD: I've missed you so, Johnny.

Next Page — **JOHN**

JOHN: I've missed you too, mother. I only have a moment to talk. I have to find my company.

MRS. GREENWOOD: I will find a place to stay in Cambridge until I can safely return to Boston.

NARRATOR 2: John left the house and ran toward the sounds of battle. They seemed to be coming from Bunker Hill. He saw signs of terror and confusion everywhere. Soldiers carried men who had been hurt during the battle. More wounded men rolled by on wagons. Their groans and cries made John's hair stand on end.

ALL BUT JOHN: [groans of pain]

JOHN: Oh, why did I enlist? Why did I think I could fight the British soldiers? They are the most powerful army in the world!

NARRATOR 1: A tall, black American soldier walked toward John. He had a wound on his neck. Blood ran down his back.

JOHN: Does it hurt?

READER 2 (AS SOLDIER): Not too much. I'm going to get a bandage put on it. Then I will return to battle.

JOHN: I need to try to act brave like that soldier.

Next Page — **NARRATOR 2**

NARRATOR 2: John continued down the road to join the fight. The battle was in Charlestown. John arrived in time to help the American militiamen, who had mostly gathered on Breed's Hill. Thousands of British soldiers began charging up the hill. The British fifers played as they charged. John and the other American fifers answered with their own battle tunes.

SOUND: [battle tunes]

NARRATOR 1: There were more British soldiers than Americans. The British also had better muskets and more of them. But the American soldiers stayed calm. Their bravery amazed John. The men obeyed the commander who said, "Don't fire until you can see the whites of their eyes."

NARRATOR 2: The Americans forced the charging British soldiers to turn back twice. The muskets sounded to John like the roll of one hundred drums. Smoke filled the air. And then the Americans ran out of gunpowder. They had to retreat. The British had won. John's company went back to Cambridge.

NARRATOR 1: One month after the battle, John stood by his tent and stared. He saw his mother rushing toward him. One of the soldiers, Sergeant Mills, was with her.

MRS. GREENWOOD: Oh, Johnny! I thought you were killed during the Battle of Bunker Hill.

NARRATOR 2: This time, John and his mother had a real visit. They talked and talked, trying to make up for the two years they were apart. Then Mrs. Greenwood kissed John good-bye.

Next Page — **MRS. GREENWOOD**

MRS. GREENWOOD: I'll be going back to Boston now. I spoke to General Washington, and he gave me a pass. My brave boy, I'm so proud of you. Sergeant Mills, what shall I tell the British in Boston when I get back home? They will probably ask me questions about you.

READER 2 (AS SERGEANT MILLS): Tell them we are ready for them at any time they choose to come and attack us.

JOHN: Yes. After the Battle of Bunker Hill, I know the American soldiers can do anything.

ALL: The End

Pronunciation Guide

Falmouth: FAL-muhth

fife: fyf

militia: mih-LIH-shuh

militiamen: mih-LIH-shuh-men

Thales: Thayls

Glossary

Breed's Hill: a hill in Charlestown, Massachusetts, where the Battle of Bunker Hill was fought

Bunker Hill: a hill in Charlestown. It is almost twice as high as Breed's Hill, but it is farther away from Boston.

Cambridge: a town in Massachusetts located six miles west of Boston

Charlestown: at the time of the American Revolution, a small village across a body of water from Boston. (Charlestown is now a neighborhood of Boston.)

colonist: someone who lived in a colony, such as one of the British colonies in North America

company: a military unit with between seventy-five and two hundred soldiers

ferryboat: a boat used to transport people and goods across a body of water

ferry keeper: a person who operates a ferry

fife: a small flute that was often played while soldiers marched, while they were at camp, and during battle

handkerchief: a square piece of cloth with many uses, including as a tissue

leave: an excused absence from military duty given by a superior officer

militia: an army of ordinary citizens

militiaman: a male militia member

musket: a gun with a long barrel

New England: at the time of the Revolution, a region in the northeastern United States that included New Hampshire, Massachusetts, Rhode Island, and Connecticut. (Maine and Vermont later became part of New England.)

tavern: a place for travelers to eat, drink, and sleep

Selected Bibliography

Greenwood, John. "A Young Patriot in the American Revolution." In *The Revolutionary Services of John Greenwood of Boston and New York, 1775–1783*, edited by Isaac J. Greenwood. New York: De Vinne Press, 1922.

Johnson, Curt. *Battles of the American Revolution.* London: Roxby Press, 1975.

McCullough, David. *1776.* New York: Simon & Schuster Press, 2005.

Werner, Emmy E. *In Pursuit of Liberty.* Westport, CT: Praeger Publishers, 2006.

Further Reading and Websites

BOOKS

Brown, Don. *Let It Begin Here, April 19, 1775.* New York: Roaring Book Press, 2008.
This book provides a lively account of how the fighting began during the Revolutionary War.

Murray, Stuart. *American Revolution*. DK Eyewitness Books series. New York: DK Publishing / Smithsonian Institution, 2005. This book combines lots of photos and interesting details about the American Revolution.

Roop, Peter, and Connie Roop. *The Top-Secret Adventure of John Darragh, Revolutionary War Spy.* Adapted by Amanda Doering Tourville. New York: Graphic Universe, 2011. Fourteen-year-old John Darragh was an American spy in British-occupied Philadelphia in 1777. In this graphic novel based on accounts of the Darragh family's spying activities for General Washington, young John undertakes a dangerous mission to deliver a message to the American army.

WEBSITES

Be a Fifer!
http://www.BeAFifer.com/
This site offers a recording of "Yankee Doodle" played by a drum and fife band (click on Philadelphia Fife and Drum). It also includes lots of facts about fifes and how to play them.

Boston 1775
http://boston1775.blogspot.com/search/label/John%20Greenwood
Historian and writer J. L. Bell has gathered interesting information about John Greenwood on this site, including a picture of the false teeth John made for George Washington!

The Coming of the American Revolution, 1764–1776
http://www.masshist.org/revolution/bunkerhill.php
The Massachusetts Historical Society gives visitors a look at the events leading up to the American Revolution. There is a great section on Bunker Hill, with accounts written by people who experienced the battle.

Dear Teachers and Librarians,

Congratulations on bringing Reader's Theater to your students! Reader's Theater is an excellent way for your students to develop their reading fluency. Phrasing and inflection, two important reading skills, are at the heart of Reader's Theater. Students also develop public speaking skills such as volume, pacing, and facial expression.

The traditional format of Reader's Theater is very simple. There really is no right or wrong way to do it. By following these few tips, you and your students will be ready to explore the world of Reader's Theater.

EQUIPMENT

Location: A theater or gymnasium is a fine place for a Reader's Theater performance, but staging the performance in the classroom works well too.

Scripts: Each reader will need a copy of the script. Scripts that are individually printed should be bound into binders that allow the readers to turn the pages easily. Printable scripts for all the books in this series are available at www.historyspeaksbooks.com.

Music Stands: Music stands are very helpful for the readers to set their scripts on.

Costumes: Traditional Reader's Theater does not use costumes. Dressing uniformly, such as all wearing the same color shirt, will give a group a polished look. Specific costume pieces can be used when a reader is performing multiple roles. They help the audience follow the story.

Props: Props are optional. If necessary, readers may mime or gesture to convey objects that are important to the story. Props can be used much like a costume piece to identify different characters performed by one reader. Prop suggestions for each story are available at www.historyspeaksbooks.com.

Background and Sound Effects: These aren't essential, but they can add to the fun of Reader's Theater. Customized backgrounds for each story in this series and sound effects corresponding to the scripts are available at www.historyspeaksbooks.com. You will need a screen or electronic whiteboard for the background. You will need a computer with speakers to play the sound effects.

PERFORMANCE

Staging: Readers usually face the audience in a straight line or a semicircle. If the readers are using music stands, the stands should be raised chest high. A stand should not block a reader's mouth or face, but it should allow for the reader to read without looking down too much. The main character is usually placed in the center. The narrator is on the end. In the case of multiple narrators, place one narrator on each end.

Reading: Reader's Theater scripts do not need to be memorized. However, the readers should be familiar enough with the script to maintain a fair amount of eye contact with the audience. Encourage readers to act with their voices by reading with inflection and emotion.

Blocking (stage movement): For traditional Reader's Theater, there are no blocking cues to follow. You may want to have the students turn the pages simultaneously. Some groups prefer that readers sit or turn their backs to the audience when their characters are "offstage" or have left a scene. Some groups will have their readers move about the stage, script in hand, to interact with the other readers. The choice is up to you.

Overture and Curtain Call: Before the performance, a member of the group should announce the title and the author of the piece. At the end of the performance, all readers step in front of their music stands, stand in a line, grasp hands, and bow in unison.

Please visit www.historyspeaksbooks.com for printable scripts, prop suggestions, sound effects, a background image that can be projected on a screen or electronic whiteboard, a Reader's Theater teacher's guide, and reading-level information for all roles.